WHAT GOES AROUND COMES AROUND

BY RICHARD McGUIRE

VIKING

She saw it fly
right by the window.

Three floors down,
they saw something
but they weren't sure what.

When he was asked
if he had seen his sister's doll,
he said "no."

The doll bounced into the street
and nearly hit a motorcycle,

which nearly hit a truck,
which slammed on its brakes.

A box fell off
and floated out to sea,

where it was spotted by a sailor,
who wondered what was in there.

Out came a bird,

who let out a honk
and woke up a monkey.

He bumped someone's elbow,
and she let go an arrow,

which startled a camel,
who booted a basket.

Out popped a snake,
who let out a hiss,

which caused a commotion,
and off fell a sultan.

He came down with a snap
and cut loose a balloon,

which sailed far away.

When it passed a parade,

it was shot by a rocket
and went down in the ocean.

It was swallowed by a whale,
who let out a burp.

A submarine shook
and let go a torpedo.

It hit a volcano,

which stirred up a wind,

which swept up an umbrella,

which came down on a rain dance.

When lightning struck,
there was a big BANG!

A plane had to swerve
to get out of the way.

The pilot saw something
but wasn't sure what.

Whatever it was
bounced into a window.

And POW!

What goes around comes around.